FLAGS

Story by Maxine Trottier
Paintings by Paul Morin

Stoddart
Kids
TORONTO • NEW YORK

Once again, for Bill
— M.T.

To Kathryn,
for starting me on this path
and for your friendship and advice
— P.M.

Text copyright © 1999 by Maxine Trottier
Illustrations copyright © 1999 by Paul Morin

We acknowledge the Canada Council for the Arts and the
Ontario Arts Council for their support of our publishing program.

Published in Canada in 1999 by
Stoddart Kids,
a division of Stoddart Publishing Co. Limited
34 Lesmill Road
Toronto, ON M3B 2T6
Tel. (416) 445-3333 Fax (416) 445-5967
E-mail Customer.Service@ccmailgw.genpub.com

Published in the United States in 1999 by
Stoddart Kids,
a division of Stoddart Publishing Co. Limited
180 Varick Street, 9th Floor
New York, New York 10014
Toll free 1-800-805-1083
E-mail gdsinc@genpub.com

Distributed in Canada by
General Distribution Services
325 Humber College Blvd.,
Toronto, ON M9W 7C3
Tel. (416) 213-1919 Fax (416) 213-1917
E-mail Customer.Service@ccmailgw.genpub.com

Distributed in the United States by
General Distribution Services
85 River Rock Drive, Suite 202
Buffalo, New York 14207
Toll free 1-800-805-1083
E-mail gdsinc@genpub.com

Canadian Cataloguing in Publication Data
Trottier, Maxine
Flags

ISBN 0-7737-3136-9

I. Morin, Paul, 1959–
II. Title.

PS8589.R685F52 1999   jC813'.54   C98-931787-0
PZ7.T76Fl 1999

Printed and bound in Hong Kong, China
By Book Art Inc., Toronto

When I was very young, I once spent a summer at my grandmother's home. Far from the flat, dry land I had always known, her house looked out over the Pacific.

The ocean sang and filled our days with the
scent of salt. A nearby river ran deep and cool.
It was a world of green and dragonflies and
fog-dampened air.

Next door to my grandmother's home was a large, white house. Mr. Hiroshi lived there. Cherry and plum trees stood at its front. My grandmother loved their smell in the spring.

The most wonderful thing
about Mr. Hiroshi's house was his
garden. Hidden by cedars and prickly
hedges, it rambled out behind his back
door. I had never seen anything like it. There
were no flower beds or ivy. No lilies or ferns
nodded their heads in the pale sunshine. Instead, it
was all sand and soft, green moss. Gravelled paths
and stepping stones wandered between the clipped

In the center lay a pond that was ringed
with small, blue irises my grandmother called
flags. Koi swam in lazy circles beneath the
water's surface. When I clapped my hands,
the fish drifted to the top and their greedy
mouths poked into the air.

I sometimes walked through the garden with Mr. Hiroshi. He would let me toss bits of bread to the fish. Even on rainy days he spent time there, moving a stone or raking the sand into perfect patterns.

"Will it ever be finished?" I asked him one day.

"I began this garden before you were born," he answered thoughtfully. "I started with one flower and a few perfect stones. Such things take time. But then a garden must begin somewhere."

Grandmother worried about Mr. Hiroshi. She had read in the newspaper that Japanese people were being taken away to camps far from their homes.

"It is because of the war, Mary," she told me. "But surely they will leave Mr. Hiroshi alone."

One morning two soldiers came with a letter to the house next door. Mr. Hiroshi would be going too.

The night before he left, we sat in his garden on a low, stone bench. The setting sun lit our faces with red and Mr. Hiroshi looked out across the ocean. I knew that Japan lay there, a world away. Behind us in the pond, the koi made tiny popping sounds as they begged for food.

"It is strange," said Mr. Hiroshi. "I was born in this country. I have lived in this house all my life. How sad that I may not be able to finish this garden."

In the morning a bus came. Many Japanese people sat inside it, their faces stiff with sadness. Grandmother and I went out to say goodbye.

"I will take care of your garden, Mr. Hiroshi," I offered.

He smiled. "That would give me great comfort, Mary," he said. "The koi are greedy, you know. Do not let them get fat."

We watched the bus drive away.

All the rest of that summer I cared for
the garden. I raked the sand and pulled small
weeds that sprouted in it. I used Mr. Hiroshi's
clippers to trim the bushes and evergreens into tidy
shapes. When I clapped my hands, the koi would rush
to the pond's surface and eat their food.

"Not too much," I scolded.

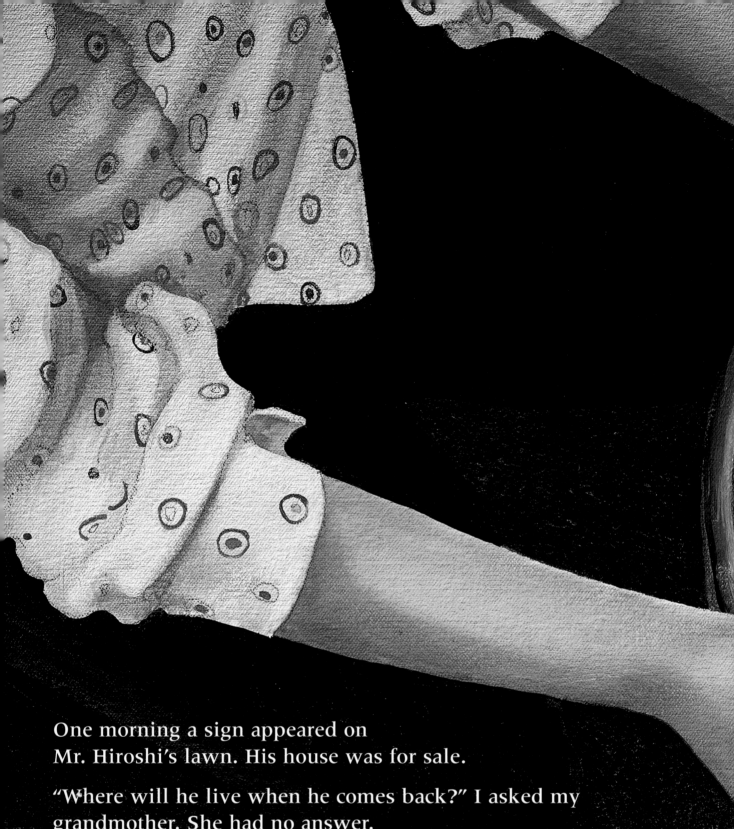

One morning a sign appeared on
Mr. Hiroshi's lawn. His house was for sale.

"Where will he live when he comes back?" I asked my
grandmother. She had no answer.

Then, the house was sold. People would move in the next day.

That night, Grandmother and I went into the garden. I knelt on
the deep moss and dug out two iris bulbs. I picked up a smooth,
flat stone and put it in my pocket. Then we netted the lazy koi
and put them in large pails of water.

Grandmother and I carried them away. We did not talk as we walked through the darkness. At the river, far from the lights of the houses and the sound of the ocean, we waded into the shallows. We tipped the pails. Slowly, river water and pond water mixed. When the koi were ready, they slipped out and disappeared.

"Maybe they will swim to Japan," I said to Grandmother.

"Maybe they will," she answered sadly.

The new people dug up Mr. Hiroshi's garden and planted grass. They filled in the pond and edged the yard with rose bushes and daisies. They seemed very pleased with their work.

In time, I returned home to my parents. Our backyard looked out onto the prairie where the wheat rippled like golden waves in a vast sea. I planted the flag bulbs in the rich, black earth and set the stone near them. I did it for Mr. Hiroshi.

It was a small thing. But then, a garden must begin somewhere.

Author's Note

Over the years, Japanese people have immigrated to North America to begin new lives. The first began to arrive in the late 1800s. They came to a culture very different from theirs in Japan. These were the *Nikkei*, people of Japanese ancestry.

They lived here for generations; many settled on the West Coast. There was a great deal of discrimination against them and life was not easy. Still, they thought they had the same rights as other citizens. Then, in 1939, World War II began. In 1941, Japan bombed Pearl Harbor in Hawaii. In Canada and the United States, the homes and businesses owned by the Nikkei were seized. Families were relocated to isolated camps or split up and sent to different places. Far from the coast, it was believed they would not be able to act as spies for Japan.

When the war ended, people of Japanese ancestry were not able to return to their homes. Many were deported to Japan, a place many had never even seen. It was years before all restrictions were removed and these people could live freely. It took a very long time, until 1988, for the Canadian and American governments to apologize for what happened to these citizens. Financial compensation was eventually made, but money cannot buy back the past; it cannot piece together lives torn apart by suspicion and racism.

It has been said that when peace comes from fear and not from the heart, it isn't really peace at all. *Flags* was written in hope that such a thing as the relocation of Japanese Canadians and Americans will never happen again. Perhaps this story will plant the seed of peace in the hearts of those who read it. And perhaps peace will grow there, much like it did long ago in Mr. Hiroshi's garden.

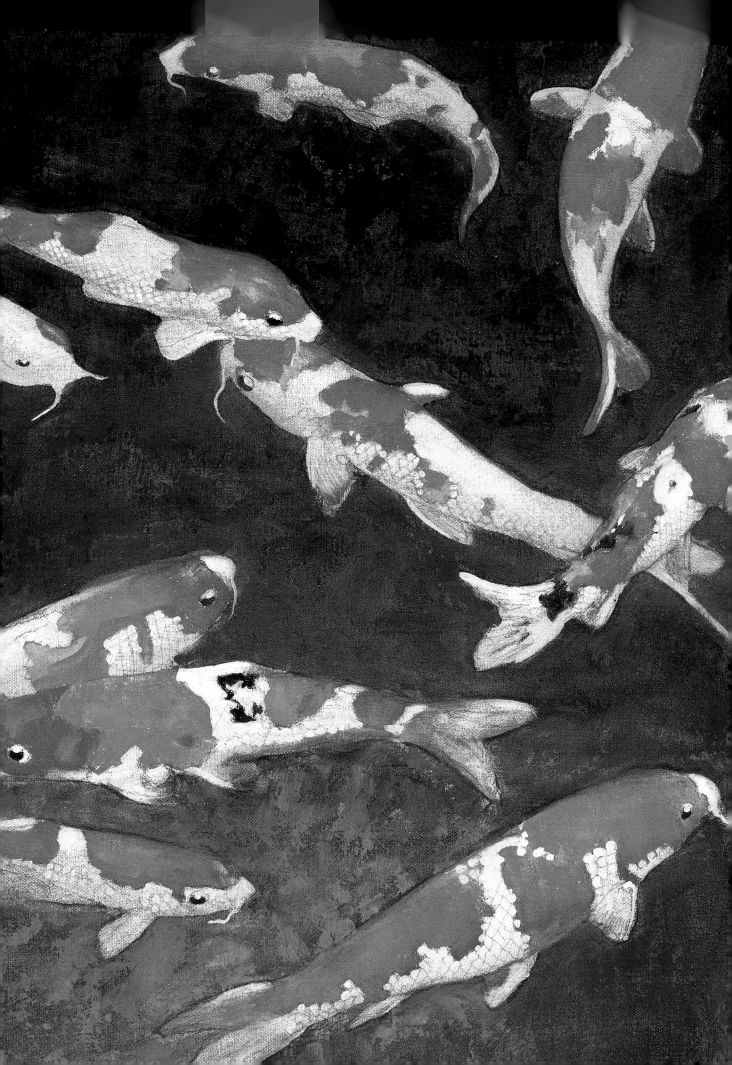